LEGO CITY

JUNGLE CHASE!

By Ace Landers
Illustrated by Paul Lee

SCHOLASTIC INC.

Deep in the LEGO® City jungle, two scientists search for a rare spider. Their team sets up camp before it gets dark.

At dinner, the crew plays a game of I Spy.
"I spy . . . DER!" yelps the photographer.
"What's a der?" asks the man scientist.
The photographer points in front of them.
"That creepy, crawly thing right over there!"

"That's what we're looking for!" cheers the woman scientist as the spider scurries away. The crew follows it into the jungle.

"Wait!" cries the photographer. "I take pictures for websites, not *spiderweb* sites!"

"Stay behind me," says the explorer. "The jungle can be dangerous."

"Are you calling us chicken?" asks the driver.

Suddenly, a giant Venus flytrap chomps down on the driver's tasty chicken leg.

"Awww!" groans the driver. "That was my dinner!"

WHEE!!

When the crew reaches a river, the spider is already on the other side.

"Well, time to go home," the photographer says. "Unless you have a boat."

But the explorer grabs a vine and tells everyone to swing across the river.

They see the spider, but they also see a sleeping leopard.

The leopard doesn't stay asleep for long.

The crew quietly runs to safety before the leopard sees them.

"Sorry," the photographer apologizes. "I'm allergic to cats."

The crew races back through the jungle until they realize the spider is nowhere to be seen.

"Where are we?" asks the driver.

"I don't know," says the explorer. "We got turned around!"

The photographer peers into a mysterious structure under a crashed plane. It leads to a dark cave. "Yuck, I bet that place is crawling with spiders."

"You're right!" agree the scientists. "Let's go!"

It is hard to see inside the cave.
The explorer turns on her flashlight.

The photographer wishes she didn't.

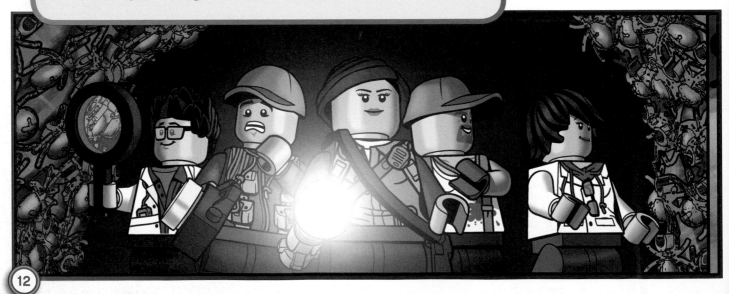

Suddenly a light flickers ahead of them. The light comes from a glowing red jewel that is sitting on a pedestal.

"Hmmm," says the photographer. "We can't leave this perfectly priceless stone in the middle of nowhere. Maybe I should bring it back with us to the city where it can be . . . appreciated."

"No," warns the explorer. "We do not know who this jewel belongs to and it is not ours to take."

"Oh, you worry too much," says the photographer. Then he grabs the jewel from its pedestal.

As soon as he takes it, a trapdoor opens up underneath the crew! They all tumble into the darkness below.

The trapdoor leads to a long twisting slide. The crew zips through the secret passageways in the heart of the jungle cave.

Finally the slide ends, leaving the crew in another part of the jungle.

"Hey, I can see our camp from here," cheers the driver.

But the spider is still missing and now the jewel is, too.

"We were so close!" the woman scientist says.

"I was so close!" says the photographer. "Now I'll never find my jewel and be rich—uh, I mean, take the jewel to a museum."

But suddenly, the explorer points at the photographer. The rare spider is on the back of his shirt!